W9-BOZ-378

LOCKED OUT

DOING RIGHT

LOCKED OUT

DOING RIGHT

PATRICK JONES

darbycreek

MINNEAPOLIS

Darby Creek
A division of Lerner Publishing Group, Inc.
241 First Avenue North
Minneapolis, MN 55401 USA

For reading levels and more information, look up this title at www.lernerbooks.com.

The images in this book are used with the permission of: © Photodisc/Getty Images (brother and sister); © iStockphoto.com/DaydreamsGirl (stone); © Maxriesgo/Dreamstime.com (prison wall) © Clearviewstock/Dreamstime.com, (prison cell).

Main body text set in Janson Text LT Std 12/17.5.
Typeface provided by Adobe Systems.

Library of Congress Cataloging-in-Publication Data

Jones, Patrick, 1961-
    Doing right / by Patrick Jones.
        pages   cm. — (Locked out)
    Summary: Puzzling over conflicting advice from family members, seventeen-year-old DeQuin Lewis continually faces trouble in his St. Paul, Minnesota, neighborhood, until a betrayal leads him to fresh start in an alternative school, one confrontation away from losing everything.
    ISBN 978-1-4677-5803-1 (lib. bdg. : alk. paper)
    ISBN 978-1-4677-6187-1 (eBook)
    [1. Conduct of life—Fiction. 2. African Americans—Fiction. 3. Prisoners' families—Fiction. 4. Fathers and sons—Fiction. 5. Uncles—Fiction. 6. Grandfathers—Fiction. 7. Saint Paul (Minn.)—Fiction.] I. Title.
PZ7.J7242Doi 2015
[Fic]—dc23   2014018197

Manufactured in the United States of America
1 – SB – 12/31/14

To Raven
—P.J.

PART ONE: SEPTEMBER

1

"You have a collect call from Oak Park Heights, will you accept the charges?" The operator's tone is flat, cold.

"Yes," I say.

"DeQuin, how you doin'?" Dad asks a few seconds later. There's noise behind him. Other voices. Prison's not a place where you go to get privacy, unless you're in solitary.

"A'right," I answer. And then there's that familiar pause of two people who have no idea what to say to each other, even though they're related.

"What you up to?" Dad asks.

"Not much. The usual."

I'm always at a loss for what to say when Dad calls. If I talk about working at KFC, Dad resents it because it reminds him that his brother—my uncle Lee—is a success, while he's a prisoner. Lee's the general manager for a string of KFCs around St. Paul. I've been working at one of 'em for almost two years. With school starting this Monday, I'll cut to twenty hours a week instead of the forty I did all summer. Still, I'll be putting a good chunk of money in the bank for college.

If I talk about school, Dad resents that too, since he'd already dropped out before tenth grade. I'd talk about a girlfriend, except I don't have one at the moment. Dad's always game to discuss females. He was a player back in the day, which is probably why my mom left. She's something else we don't talk about.

"Me and Martel and Anton are 'bout to head to Valleyfair," I say. Just to be saying something. And also so that Dad will know my friends are waiting on me. They're in the kitchen right now, putting up with Gramps and his stories.

In fact, I can hear Gramps from the other room: "Why you boys dressed like that? Pants hanging down like that. Show some respect for yourselves . . . "

"Good, good," says Dad. He's heard all about Martel and Anton, even though he's never met 'em. The three of us have been cruising around together since we were in kindergarten, 'bout the same time Dad started his life sentence. Usually, when I can't think of much to talk to Dad about, I'll talk about Martel and Anton. Not this time, though. Lately I'm getting the sense that Martel and Anton only care about living day to day, and if I hang with them much longer, I'll be retracing Dad's footsteps.

So...more silence. Like those gray walls that stand between Dad and me have somehow made their way into the phone lines.

"When you coming to visit?" He makes his questions sound like orders.

"Soon." Whenever Uncle Lee decides to take me. Usually it's every few months, but Lee's been working a lot lately, hasn't had much time off. And since I'm still only seventeen, I can't go on my own. Even if I wanted to. Which I'm not sure I do.

I hate these calls. They're just reminders that Dad and I barely know each other. And that's another thing I can't talk to him about: the reason we're strangers.

It's not just because he killed a guy in some messed-up gang stuff. He could've done less time, he said, if he snitched on his squad, but "real men protect their own." So he saved guys who wore the same colors from doing time, and he left his five-year-old son without a father.

"Well—my time's 'bout up, DeQuin. You take care."

"OK," I say. "You too."

It's how we always end these calls. It fits. Dad never took care of me, but he expects me to take care of myself.

Anyway, I'm glad the call's over. Unlike Dad, I've got places to be.

2

"He pulled out a gun!" Gramps yells as I walk into the kitchen. Martel and Anton have been stuck at the table with Gramps while I was talking to Dad.

"Was it a choppa?" Martel asks Gramps, who gives him a blank look. I see that look a lot.

Martel sighs, tries again. "What kind of gun was it?"

"A shotgun if I recollect, but that's not important," Gramps continues. "What's important is you boys knowing what happened that day in Selma."

"Can we bounce?" I ask Gramps. I've heard this story a hundred times: Gramps walking

across some bridge in Alabama back in the six-
ties, part of some big civil rights march, and
getting the crap beat out of him by the police. I
could tell it in my sleep.

I slip in my ear buds and head for the door.
But Gramps gives me that stern, cop-like
"freeze" glare, so I pause.

"Mr. Jimmie Lee Jackson was a deacon at my
church in Marion, Alabama," Gramps says. "And
they shot him dead in 1965 for trying to vote."

"And that led to the Selma protest march
and you seeing Dr. King." I try to move the
story along. "And that's why Dad's name is Jimmie and why Uncle Lee's name is Lee."

Gramps isn't pleased at my interruption.
"You should listen more, talk less, DeQuin."

It's been like this all summer, ever since
Gramps got sick and moved up from Alabama
to live with Uncle Lee and me. Nothing but
complaining about everything. Mostly about
me.

"And you should take those things out of
your ears when I'm talking to you." He points at
my buds like they're illegal. "I don't understand

why you all have to always be listening to that music. Glorifying guns and criminals. Using that word. Disrespecting black women..."

I cut him off. "Wait a second. You said *'you all* listen to.' What do you mean by that?"

"You know what I mean," Gramps says. "You young people."

I could argue with him. We argue a lot, Gramps and me. He's got it in his head that everyone my age is looking for trouble. I guess Martel and Anton won't do much to change his mind. Like Dad, they're easing into the fast flow of the streets.

And me?

I don't know.

Uncle Lee's always telling me that with my good grades, I could get into college easy—even get a scholarship to help pay for it. He sees me getting some fancy business degree, following in his footsteps instead of in Dad's.

I'm not sure I want a life like Lee's. He's always working, always stressed. Always trying not to get on his boss's bad side or make a mistake that could get him in trouble.

But I *know* I don't want a life like Dad's.

And I know I don't have time to get into it with Gramps right now. "OK, we're out," I say. "Those roller coasters don't run all night."

"Shouldn't you two be working?" Gramps asks Martel and Anton. "Don't you boys have jobs like DeQuin?"

They work, but not at jobs they'd tell him about. "Yeah, fry me some chicken, DeQuin," Anton says.

"With a side of taters," Martel adds. They laugh loud and long like they're high already.

"That chicken is going to pay for DeQuin's college," Gramps says. "Hard work turns that fried chicken right into tuition. I worked in the steel mills to pay for my son Lee's college, no shame in working to pay your way..."

"Let's goooo," I say and motion for Martel and Anton to join me. Martel gets out the keys to his ride, a three-year-old Jeep that's way nicer than my ancient Corolla.

"One more thing, DeQuin," says Gramps.
"Yeah?"

He pounds his cane hard on the kitchen floor.

"Pull up your dang pants!" We laugh, since he says it all the time. Sagging, so they say, started in prisons and spread to the outs. I don't know if that's true. I'll have to ask Dad.

3

"She's fine, go talk to her!" Martel pokes me in the side. We stand together outside the Demon Drop ride at the amusement park. On the last Saturday night of summer vacation, it's packed, mostly with people our age, but not so much our color.

"Let it go," I say, trying not to look at the cute white girl a few feet away. She stands with two friends, also white. They pass a phone around, laughing loud.

"Three of us, three of them. Do the math, Einstein." Anton adds his poke in my side. They're always calling me Einstein. I get good grades at school, even made honor roll last year as a sophomore, so they're always ragging on me.

"Then you talk to 'em, Anton," I snap back.

"Raquel would kill me!" I let that go. I know he's cheated on her before, not that it's any of my business. Me, I don't go that route. I prefer one girl at a time.

"But that doesn't mean we can't party with 'em," Anton adds. "Come on, it's almost midnight, they're about to close up. It's now or never."

"DeQuin, don't be a coward," says Martel. "Run up there. We know you like the ladies, and ladies like you plenty."

"You crazy, Martel." But it's the truth. While I don't have a girlfriend right now, that's normally not the case. I guess being tall and "fine," as the girls always say, tends to work out well for me.

"How many times you hooked up with a white girl?" Martel asks.

"That don't matter none."

"Then help a brother out," Martel says, and then pushes me hard toward the three girls.

"My cuz thinks you're fine," I tell the shortest of the girls, since Martel is only 5'5. He seems even shorter because he hangs with two six-footers. "What's your name?"

The short girl doesn't look pleased. The tallest one says, "Her name is Brittney."

I laugh. Seems every third white girl who ever works at KFC is named Brittney. Brittney whispers for her friend to shut up. I point back at my boys. "That's Martel."

"What's *your* name?" the tall one asks, ignoring her friend's glare.

"DeQuin Lewis, Harding High School, St. Paul, Minnesota," I answer. "And where are you all from?" I notice Brittney wears an oversize varsity jacket from Woodbury, better known with us as Whitebury. Before the tall girl can answer, the third girl tugs on her arm.

"Chelsea, let's go," third girl whispers.

"Chelsea and Brittney and whoever, nice to meet you," I say. "If you three want to—"

"We have to go," third girl says, aiming her words at me, not her friends. Behind me, I hear Martel and Anton laughing like little kids on Christmas morning.

"Hit me up online," I say to Chelsea, she of

the long brown hair and ice-blue eyes. "Tell your friends not to worry. I'm a'right. I don't bite—that is, unless you want me to."

Chelsea rolls her pretty blue eyes, laughs, and starts to walk away.

"Hey, what's up?"

Three big white guys come up behind the girls. They all have shaved short hair like football players wear during the season. Two of them have on varsity jackets loaded with letters. All three are cupping super-sized sodas in their paws.

"These guys bothering you, Brit?" asks the tallest guy, the one without a varsity jacket. Tiny Brittney glances at him, then back at me.

"We were just talking," I say, already backing away. "It's all good."

But now Anton and Martel have come closer. Anton marches up to the tall guy and gets right in his face, nose to nose. So close I wonder if the guy's gonna get a contact high.

"You got some problem with us?" Anton says.

"Anton, let's just go," I say. I reach for his arm, but he pulls it away.

"Shut up, Barack!" one of the other guys snaps at me.

"What did you say?" And it's on. Back and forth, jaw to jaw, each of us bust out our A+ insult game, except I'm way too quick for these fools.

"...And another thing—"

"If you want to fight, Barack"—the guy pushes me in the chest—"let's fight!"

If I was Grandpa, I'd take his crap. If I was Dad, I'd clean his clock. If I was Lee, I'd just walk away.

He pushes me again.

I break my stare and take a quick look around the amusement park. The odds aren't fair. A fight won't end well. From the corner of my eye I see two security guys—one white, one black—running at us. There's not going to be a fight, but I can still put some fear into these idiots.

"You sure about that?" I raise my shirt so he can see the top of the object tucked in the waistband of my boxers. In the dark, I'm betting that all he can see is a black bulging shape. "You sure you want what I'm packing?"

The big guy slaps his friend's arm and motions for him to look at me. As soon as they get a glimpse, I put my shirt down. The Woodburys head east, we head west. It's over.

When the security guards catch up to us, my heart's booming like a bass riff. "How's it going, boys?" the white guard asks.

"What's the problem?" adds the black guard with just as much "I'm in charge" attitude.

In the background, I hear loud screams from the top of the coaster. "What's *your* problem?" I shoot back. Martel and Anton look all stunned. Normally I let stuff go. I don't want to be a hothead like my dad, getting into trouble and going to jail, but something about these guys bothers me. Why they hassling us and not the kids from Whitebury?

"We don't need any trouble tonight, guys," the black guard says. "As a matter of—"

The white guard cuts him off. "Why don't you boys head back home?"

It's one thing when Gramps calls us boys. This is different.

For a split second I think about taking a step

closer to him. Getting up in his face. Saying "Do I look like a *boy* to you now?"

But I know it's not a good idea to mess with the wannabe cops. Even Martel and Anton have better sense than that.

I spit on the ground and walk away.

4

Martel and Anton are laughing about the guards as we exit the park and make our way to Martel's Jeep.

"Did you see the look—" is as far as Anton gets before we see the three guys from Woodbury standing in the emptying parking lot.

"Keep walking," I say.

"No, let's do this," Martel says. "They're big, but I messed up bigger dudes than them."

"Martel, ain't worth it," I say, trying to keep my voice calm even when inside I'm feeling anything but. "School starts Monday. I don't want to spend a night in jail."

"It ain't so bad," Martel says. Both he and

Anton got arrested for distribution, but after a few nights in juvie, they got put on ankle bracelet. Martel talks about spending time at JDC like it's something to be proud of, which I don't get. Maybe if he'd spent his childhood looking at his dad through a glass partition, he'd feel different.

"It'll be worse for them," Anton says. "They'll spend the night in a hospital."

I trail behind, not sure what to do. Unlike them or Dad, I've never been in a serious fight. My smart mouth got me close a few times, but I normally bluff my way out of it like I did in the park. I don't think that's going to work again. If my friends fight, then do I follow?

"You with us, DeQuin?" Martel asks with attitude in his voice like I got no choice. A few months ago, there was no need to ask. But it's hard to follow someone when you know you're headed in different directions. I say nothing. They're running on something almost primal. They got challenged, and everything in their experience tells them to fight back.

"I don't have—" Martel says right before he

gets tackled by two white guys in varsity jackets. Anton gets decked from the side too. The three guys from earlier are still in front of us. Turns out they got backup.

As Martel and Anton fight off the guys who jumped them, the three original guys run toward me.

And I run away faster than whoever runs the hundred-meter on the Harding track team.

I zigzag through the parking lot. The headlights cast shadows around me. The three guys call me a coward and few other names, but they give up the chase pretty quick.

I keep running until I reach the edge of the parking lot. I duck behind a car to catch my breath, close my eyes, and clutch my stomach.

From the park, I hear the last screams from the last ride of summer coming from the coasters.

Soon, I pretend not to hear other sounds. Sirens. Police car. Ambulance.

And I pretend not to hear the voice in the back of my head. It's my dad calling me a coward.

Dad never ran away from a fight. He's always

been proud of that. Of course, it got him a life of walls and bars, while I'm walking free. What he thinks shouldn't matter to me.

But I can't get that voice out of my head.

I pull up my shirt, put my hand on the black object in my waistband and take it out. I hold it tight until my hand stops shaking, then press down.

"Uncle Lee, I need your help," I say into my new big-ass phone.

5

"So that's what happened," I say to Uncle Lee just as we're getting on 35E toward St. Paul. In the time it took him to come get me at the park in Shakopee, I rehearsed how I'd tell the story. Like I expected, he interrupted with lots of questions, grunts, and sighs. Now he's silent for a second, deciding which of those to throw at me next.

"So you called me instead of calling the police?" he asks finally.

"You think that's what I should've done?"

"Absolutely. You gotta be careful, DeQuin. Minnesota's got the conceal and carry law now. Those boys could've had guns. You run into trouble like this, you should never try to deal with it on your own. It could've gotten much uglier."

I'm still seeing those guys tackling Anton and Martel. I don't want to think about how much worse it could've been.

"Well, the cops did show up," I tell my uncle. "I heard the sirens."

"Yeah, a little late. Have you tried to call Anton or Martel?"

"No." I have no idea what I'd say to them. Sorry won't cut it. "You think they got arrested?" I keep telling myself I ran not because I was scared of getting hurt, but because I didn't want to get in trouble.

"If they did, they had it coming. That's it— that's the last straw with those two. I don't want you hanging around with them anymore."

I almost breathe a sigh of relief. Now it's not my fault if I avoid them. I can blame my uncle. "But they're my friends," I argue back, putting up a false front.

"They used to be your friends," Lee says, all stern and gruff. "They're magnets for trouble. You follow them, and you're going to get into trouble like your dad. I raised you better than that. You're not losing everything I worked so hard for because of your hoodlum friends. I already got to visit my brother in prison, I'm not going to be visiting his son that I'm raising. No sir, no sir."

Gramps is up when we get home. Lee tells me I should let Gramps know what happened, since he was worried too. I sit at the kitchen table while Lee escapes into his office. I keep my hand in my pocket on my phone, but it doesn't ring.

Gramps makes me tell the whole story over again. I leave out some of the parts, just like I did with Lee, but all the time I'm talking, Gramps is shaking his head like he's trying to screw in his neck.

"Don't you know nothing about history, DeQuin?" he says when I'm done.

I shrug.

"You never heard about Emmett Till? Don't they teach you nothing in school no more?"

Another shrug.

"He was a black boy who talked to a white

woman in Mississippi back in the 1950s, and then he turned up dead. They arrested the rednecks who done it. Everybody known they'd done it, but like I said, it was Mississippi and an all-white jury, so they got off. It was just another lynching."

"It's not like that anymore."

He's back to screwing in his neck with the head shakes. "You tell that to the white boys who jumped you tonight."

"Look, Gramps, we weren't bothering those girls. We talked to 'em for like thirty seconds, then we were gonna leave 'em alone. You telling me I should just avoid all white people all the time in case I piss off some stupid football player?"

"Of course not," snaps Gramps. "You think that's what I was fighting for on that bridge in Selma? Let me tell you, DeQuin, they beat us on that bridge, but we never backed down. We showed everybody we was stronger even though we took a beating."

"So what—you saying I should've just let myself get beat up?"

"I'm saying sometimes you find yourself up against a wall, and running ain't the answer. Running and hiding won't save you. Sometimes a man's got to stand his ground." He pounds his cane as punctuation.

"So you don't think I should've called the police?" I don't tell him that was Lee's advice.

Gramps groans. "Who do you think it was beating us up on the Pettus Bridge in Selma?"

"Man, those were some hard times," I say real soft, trying to calm him down.

"But we got through it, and you know why we did it?" Gramps asks. He seems less testy now. "We did it for our kids, their kids. We stood our ground and took those beatings for you."

I got no idea what to say to that, so I go with, "Thanks, Gramps."

Gramps nods, staring hard at me. "So don't blow it by acting like some fool."

"I won't," I say—even though I still don't know what's most foolish: to fight, to flee, or to freeze.

6

"Hey, DeQuin, you heard about Anton and Martel?" Rashad asks me at lunch on the first day of school. The four of us always sat together last year—that is, when Anton and Martel actually showed up. Rashad's getting into sports and pulling away from Anton and Martel, so I guess we're becoming better friends. It's easier to say "no" when you got some backup.

I shake my head. "What's up?" I ask.

"They're in jail in Scott County," Rashad says around a mouthful of pizza. "I saw Martel on Saturday and he said for sure he was coming back to school. So when he didn't show this morning, I texted my moms to have her ask his moms, and now I got the whole story."

It's just like I figured. Everybody at Harding's gonna hear how I ran.

"They got into some big rumble at Valleyfair on Saturday night. I thought you was supposed to be with them? I had to work."

I take a bite of my leftover KFC sandwich and ask another question so I don't have to lie. "Why they still in jail?"

"His moms said 'cause that's the only thing they know how to do with black people in Scott County." I laugh probably louder than I should.

"But for real," says Rashad, "they had a record, plus a bag with a little weed in it." In other words the usual thing you'd find in their pockets.

"Who'd they fight? What happened them?" I ask, making sure not to let on I know anything.

"My moms said they're probably out, 'cause they're white."

"Glad they're not hurt at least. Hit me up if you hear anything else."

"Martel's moms said they should be back

on Friday—that's if school takes 'em back. But if they kicked out every brother that done time, this place would be half empty." I don't say anything, just focus on chewing on my cold chicken sandwich.

Part of me's relieved that Martel and Anton aren't hurt bad. But part of me's wondering what to expect on Friday.

If we're still friends—if that's what matters to them—they'll give me crap about it, but that's all.

But if they play by the rules of the street, they gotta teach me a lesson. A lesson I earned.

***

As soon as I get off the bus from school on Thursday, I see Martel's Jeep rounding the corner. It pulls up next to me. The bass is turned up, and the windows are almost shaking. When the driver's side window rolls down, it's like my ears have just been sucker punched.

"Get in, DeQuin," Martel says. He must see me hesitate, because right away he adds, "Get in, it's all good. We cool."

I open the door, throw my bag in, and hop in the backseat. I do it fast just in case Lee's home and happens to be looking out the window, since he told me I needed to steer clear of Anton and Martel. I've broken up with girls before, but never with guy friends. It's gonna feel weird.

I shout over the music. "About Valleyfair—"

Martel and Anton turn around. They look all stern at me, then laugh and offer me a bump. Both of them still got bandages on their noses, and Martel's got a big ugly pink Band-Aid on his forehead and a puffy left eye.

"You wanna explain it?" Martel says, turning his back to me and driving off. With the music loud, I got to shout over it. I'd ask him to turn it down, but he doesn't owe me any favors.

"I didn't know what to do!" I yell. I've thought about what I'd say when they confronted me, but the music—and weed smoke—is throwing me off. They don't offer me a hit.

"Thing is, DeQuin, I don't think this thing is over," Martel says.

"What do you mean?" I ask.

"I saw a pickup truck behind us with

Woodbury High bumper stickers," Martel says.

"I saw that too," Anton adds. He points at the side mirror. I don't see anything.

"Here's your chance to man up, DeQuin," Martel says and then hits the gas. He drives fast but safe toward one of the industrial parks.

"Maybe this time the odds will be even," Anton says.

"Except this time we won't be flashing no phone pretending it's a .22," Martel says and then makes a hard right into an empty parking lot behind what looks like a vacant building.

He stops the car fast, and my chest crashes hard against the seat. If they're right about the Woodbury guys following us, I'm guessing it won't be the only pain I'll be feeling. I should've just pretended not to hear him and not got in the car. I ran away before, but now I'm in a worse situation.

"Get out, let's do this," Martel says. Anton yells his approval.

I climb out of the car. "You see them, DeQuin?" Anton asks. He points at the road.

"I don't see nothing."

"Look harder, Einstein," Martel suggests, so I do.

I take another step away from the Jeep right before something cracks into the back of my skull.

PART TWO: JANUARY / FEBRUARY

7

"Welcome to Armstrong High School, DeQuin," says Mrs. Oliver, the principal, all smiles.

"Thanks," I mumble. I cover my eyes to block out what seems to be a blinding light. Ever since I came out of the coma in December, bright lights and loud noises give me killer headaches.

"We really appreciate you taking DeQuin into your school," says Lee, who is all suited up. "Harding isn't an option anymore, and with DeQuin's challenges since..."

And he stops. We don't talk about "since." Since I got jumped by a bunch of kids from Woodbury, according to Anton and Martel.

Somehow they fought them off, they said, yet still I got hurt bad: broken jaw, concussion, busted eardrum, and other stuff I don't remember.

"We'll accommodate DeQuin as best we can," Mrs. Oliver says. "We'll do an IEP."

"IEP?" asks Gramps, who insisted on coming with us.

"Individualized education plan," she answers. She doesn't say it's code for special ed.

"I don't understand," Gramps says, his normal response to the modern world. While Mrs. Oliver explains, I'm thinking about Harding. Lee says my old school's not safe for me, but I can't tell if he really believes that or if he just wants to get me away from Martel and Anton. Either way, he wouldn't take any arguments from me. So now it's Armstrong, in the burbs, over in Oakdale. Good thing is I get to drive to school every day.

"Is there anything else, Mr. Lewis, that I could help you with?" she asks.

Lee asks a bunch more questions, since obviously he's Mr. Lewis and I'm not. When there's a break, I ask something important to me. "Are there any other students from Harding here?"

"A few," says Mrs. Oliver. "You might see some old friends."

That wipes the smile off Lee's face. "Better that he make some new ones."

Not only are Anton and Martel off limits, so is everyone I used to hang with, except people Uncle Lee approves. I'm a little boy again.

"One last question," Gramps says. "What are you doing for Black History Month?"

Mrs. Oliver jumps right into another spiel. "At Armstrong, we make a point to celebrate the diversity of our student body," she says. I try not to laugh, since I didn't see too many brown faces in the Armstrong hallways when we got here.

"I was at the march on Selma," Gramps says. I thought this meeting was about me, but no. "I think it would be good for young people to hear how it was back in the day, when we were fighting for our civil rights. I got lots of stories."

Mrs. Oliver's face lights up. "I can certainly arrange that, sir."

Gramps smiles whenever anybody calls him sir. "Thank you, ma'am."

I pull up my hood, trying to block out some of

8

Mrs. Oliver hands me off to a hipster white science teacher like I'm a relay baton or something. She gives him some papers, wishes me luck, and walks away.

"DeQuin, welcome to environmental science," the guy says, never looking up from the papers. "Why don't you take a seat anywhere there's space available?"

I quick-scan the room. The desks are pushed together into groups of four. In one of the clusters closest to the front, I see a girl rocking a pink zip hoodie with a white beater underneath that she fills out fine. Dark brown skin, almost sparkling thick lips, and intense focus. The only thing I don't like about her is there's no empty seat next to her.

"I need to sit close to the front, I got a busted eardrum so I don't hear too well," I tell the teacher.

"Sure thing," he says. "Just grab a chair for today." I take an extra chair from the back and set it down right next to the pink-hoodie girl's desk. The teacher starts talking about climate change, but I've got other types of science on my mind, like animal attraction and magnetic pull.

I open a notebook, but then pretend I don't have anything to write with, so I whisper to the hoodie girl. "You got a pen or something?"

She makes this little sniff sound and reaches behind her ear. She hands me a pen from beneath relaxed shiny shoulder-length hair.

"Thanks. I'm DeQuin," I whisper. "And you are?"

"Smooth, DeQuin, real smooth," she says, but doesn't give up her name.

I keep waiting for another chance to say something to this girl, but the teacher keeps talking like if he shuts his mouth, he's going to die. Finally he tells us to talk at our tables about something. I agree with everything the mystery girl says, and she says a lot. Smart too. Somebody else in our group calls her Ralisha. So now at least I've got her name.

When the bell rings, I go to hand her back her pen. "Thanks again."

"Keep it." She picks up her books, then stands. I try not to stare, but it's hard. She fills out her jeans as fine as she does the beater.

"Thanks," I say and then flash my A+ smile. She kind of smiles back. "Why?"

"Why what?" she asks.

"Why do you want me to keep your pen?" I ask just to keep the conversation going.

"So you'll have one when I decide to give you my phone number."

I pull out my phone. "How about now?"

"How about you slow down?"

"You never know how many days you got." I show her the scar on the back of my head.

"You must not be much of a fighter," she says jokingly.

"You should see the other guys." I wish she *could* see the other guys and tell me who they

9

To get from east St. Paul to Oak Park Heights takes us right by the Maplewood Mall and through Whitebury. Even as I see the city limit sign, I think of the guys from the amusement park. Like they're lying in wait for me here.

If you had a map of our drive, it'd look like an Oreo from the side: leaving black-heavy east St. Paul, driving through the wide white burbs, and ending up at the prison. More black people live in Oak Park Heights than most Minnesota towns.

The prison is max security and so is the visiting. It's three of us on one side of the heavy glass, Dad on the other side.

Gramps starts upbeat, but gets grumpy pretty quick. Lee comes mainly to be there for me, like he always is. He's got nothing much to say to Dad. Hasn't for years. Lee took the hard way, Dad took the easy way. It doesn't take a genius to do the math and see where those choices landed them.

After barely a minute, Lee hands me the phone. "How you doin', DeQuin?" Dad asks, like always, like he cares. At least he pretends to care.

I tell him I'm doing better. This is the first time we've talked since right after I got released from the hospital. I was still pretty out of it then.

"You seen Martel and Anton at all?" Dad asks now.

I shake my head. "Nah. Not since it happened."

That last call, I told him the whole story, everything that went down with Martel and Anton. Funny thing, I can't lie to my dad, never could. Maybe that's why I'd never make it as a criminal. I'm an honest person, somehow.

"Still can't believe you ran," Dad says, shaking

his head. "If I was out, I'd teach you how to fight, how to be a man, not a coward."

I try not to react. But it's a kick in the balls. Every time I come here, I tell myself that it doesn't matter what he says because of what he's done with his life. And I believe it until I hear his voice and look into his face. It's my face. He's part of me no matter what.

10

"So I guess I should start when I was just a boy in Alabama," Gramps says. He sits on a stool in the front of the room talking to my mostly white history class about Black History.

"Wherever you would like to start, Mr. Lewis," the history teacher, Mr. Hart, says.

I lean in to listen, but also so I can sneak a peek at Ralisha.

Gramps talks about growing up in Alabama, going to a black-only school, separate drinking fountains, all of it. Hard to believe that happened in the lifetime of somebody who lives in my house. Why did people put up with that crap for so long?

Mr. Hart notices some people falling asleep, so he asks a question. "Who can tell me about Brown versus Board of Education?"

Not a hand goes up. I know the answer, but I'm trying not to be a show-off. I just want to blend in here, not make enemies, find a few friends.

"Nobody knows about Brown versus Board of Education?" Mr. Hart asks, all stunned.

"Last night I watched the movie *Freddy vs. Jason*," this girl Tia says.

She gets a laugh, but Ralisha rolls her eyes and mutters, "Just listen."

Gramps looks frustrated and confused, so I save him.

"That was the Supreme Court case that ended segregated schools in the United States," I say—trying to act casual, not all "Einstein," as Martel and Anton would say. I notice Ralisha crack a little bit of a smile when I get serious.

"That's right, DeQuin," Gramps says. "And one of the lawyers involved in that case, Thurgood Marshall, later went on to become the first African American Supreme Court Justice."

"What kind of name is Thurgood?" Tia snickers. Gramps looks like he got slapped.

"What kind of name is Tia?" Ralisha snaps.

"Kind of name my boo likes whispering in my ear," Tia hisses. "You wouldn't know nothin' 'bout that since Tobias dropped your—"

"*I* dropped *him!*" Ralisha cuts across her. "Now shut up and listen to the man talk."

"Girl, Tobias just didn't want no more of your ugly face and fat ass."

"Shut your mouth or I'm shutting it for you!" Ralisha yells.

Tia pushes her chair over and starts toward Ralisha, who meets her halfway. Mr. Hart tries to get between the two girls, but he doesn't have much luck keeping them apart. Tia and Ralisha keep screaming at each other even as they're throwing hands. A hard slap bloodies Ralisha's nose, and that's what unfreezes me.

I rocket to the front of the room and grab Gramps's arm. "Gramps, get out of the way," I say and then lead him to the door.

He starts to protest, but I got no time to argue with him. It's time for action. Once he's safe from the fray, I push my way through the circle that's formed around the girls almost like a cage.

"Enough!" Mr. Hart keeps repeating louder each time, but he should save his words.

Tia's got bigger, stronger, tougher, and faster hands, so I make my move. I grab Ralisha, pinching her flailing arms against her sides. I pick her up and carry her to the back of the room.

"Let go!" she screams. No tears, but blood drips down from her nose, staining my gray hoodie. She's squirming and kicking her legs, but I just hold her tighter.

"Stay out of this, DeQuin!" Tia yells from across the room, but she's cut off by Mrs. Oliver's commanding voice. Our principal stands in the doorway and tells everyone to sit down. She's got two rental cops as backup.

Slowly the room calms down as the rental cops escort Tia and Ralisha from the room.

I go over to check on Gramps. "You OK?" He nods. "Sorry about that."

"You really jumped into action there," he says.

I can't tell from his tone if he thinks that was a smart or stupid thing to do. I don't get a chance to ask him before Mr. Hart brings Gramps back to the front of the room. Then Gramps goes back to talking about nonviolence, preaching to the deaf ears of kids who live in an eye-for-an eye world.

11

"DeQuin, please sit," Mrs. Oliver says. Sitting next to her is Mrs. Washington, the special ed teacher I haven't seen since we did my IEP the second day.

"What did I do wrong?" I ask.

"We were already planning on having this check-in," Mrs. Oliver says, smiles. "I don't want you to assume the only time you ever get called into my office is because you've done something wrong. I don't want you to associate me, this office, or even this school with failure. Understand?"

I nod and take off my hood, exposing my shaved head. I want them to see my scar.

"But first, yes, we need to address the fight the other day in Mr. Hart's classroom and—"

I cut her off. "I didn't start it. I was trying to end it."

"That's what Mr. Hart said, but you shouldn't do that. You could've gotten hurt yourself."

"Ain't no female ever gonna hurt me," I say, which is a total lie. Normally I break up with girls first so they can't say they dumped me. It's about knowing when to flee.

"Still, it's not a good idea to involve yourself in any fights," Mrs. Oliver says. "In starting them or ending them. Let the staff handle it, OK, DeQuin?"

"The other thing we want to discuss is progress on your IEP," Mrs. Washington says. "I'd asked your uncle to join us this morning, but it looks as if something came up at work."

"Wouldn't be the first time," I say—then wish I hadn't. Lee's always been there for me as much as he can. He saved me from a life in foster care and took me into his home. He wants the best for me, even if his version of the best is mostly about hard work, sacrifice, compromise, and all those other words he always uses.

"We'll find another time. Caregivers are important to the process," Mrs. Washington says. "The issues you came here with as a result of your concussion—short-term memory loss, light sensitivity, and so on—seem to be going away, which is consistent with that kind of injury."

"My head don't hurt as much either and my hearing's all the way back, too."

"That's good. Now just stay out of trouble," Mrs. Oliver says as she writes the pass for me to go back to class. I don't tell her that trouble seems to find me far too easy. I wonder if it was like that for my dad too.

***

I get back to science class just as it's ending. "What did I miss?" I ask Ralisha—who, much to my surprise, didn't get suspended after the fight. Tia's still in school too, not that I care.

She opens up her purse and pulls out a pad of pink Post-it notes. "Gimme your hand."

I hold out my left hand.

"Thanks for sticking up for me other day."

"You were the one sticking up for my gramps when Tia made fun of him."

"Yeah, and then I made a fool of myself. I try to stay out of drama like that, but when I'm getting whopped I gotta put up a fuss about it. You did good, getting me to settle down, making sure nobody got hurt."

In my palm, Ralisha places a pink sticky note with the handwritten number six on it. "If you act like a gentleman for nine more days in a row, DeQuin, then you'll get all ten of my digits."

12

"What time you off work?" I ask Ralisha. I'm waiting with her by the bus stop during lunch hour. Just like every day, she's headed home after morning classes. She does online school the rest of the day. I don't ask why and she ain't saying.

"Nine. You?"

"Ten thirty, it sucks," I reply. "But how else are we getting money for college?"

She raises her eyebrows at me. That girl has some fine, sassy eyebrows. "So you're gonna go to college, DeQuin?"

"That's the plan," I say. It's Uncle Lee's plan, and Gramps's plan, and more and more it feels like mine.

"Huh," is all she says. Then she shivers. I wrap my arms around her. It took ten days, but I got her digits, her attention, and her lips on mine.

"Maybe we could hang out or something afterward." I blow on my hands to warm them and then put them on her freezing face. She warms my mouth with a kiss.

"Or something," she says.

It's not the answer I was hoping for. So far, she won't see me outside of school. But I don't push. Instead I say, "Can I ask you a question?"

She looks at her phone. "Make it quick, bell's gonna ring and you don't wanna be late."

"What happened with that guy Tobias? The dude Tia mentioned that day in history class."

She raises those eyebrows again. "Does it matter?"

"I was just wondering because I don't want to make the same mistake," I say, super nice.

She laughs at that. "Look, I broke up with him because there was too much childish drama. I'm a serious person with plans and he was just a fool."

"I'm a serious person too," I say, but can't help

smiling, which I do whenever I'm around her.

"I don't know yet if you're serious enough for me to get serious with," Ralisha says.

"Come on now," I say. "I'm the kind of boy you could bring home to mom and dad."

"Why do you think I want you to meet my family?" she asks.

I try to figure out how to pull my size-12 out of my mouth. "No reason. I'm sorry. I didn't mean nothing by it." She never talks about her family, but then again, neither do I.

"You see, there you go, backing up. Give some of that back. Say 'Ralisha, you ain't exactly a mom's dream date for her son!'" For somebody wanting serious, she's pretty funny.

"I don't have a mom, so no worries," I say. I'm playing, but the words come out wrong. A little sad, a little angry.

"I'm sorry, DeQuin." She's quiet for a second, then asks, "You got a dad?"

"Sort of."

I'm trying to decide how much to say, but Ralisha doesn't push me. "Well, I know you got a grandpa, and I bet he would straight up have a heart attack if he knew you're going out with one of those crazy girls who went at it in the middle of his talk."

"That's for sure," I laugh.

But I'm thinking about other girlfriends I've had—and dumped. Run away from. There's no doubt in my mind that some of them think of me the way Ralisha thinks of Tobias. And they got good reasons. I ain't never been with the same girlfriend longer than a couple months. Never tried to build something that could last.

I gotta change that. And Ralisha can't ever learn about the boy I was until I become the man I want to be.

13

It's Valentine's Day, and business is dead. So the boss—who reports to Lee—lets me go home early. I head over to the Maplewood Mall, where Ralisha works at Foot Locker.

Ralisha's surprised to see me when she comes out after her shift. "DeQuin, what you doing here?"

"I just thought we could hang out or something now that you're done with work."

"Look, my parents are real strict about me coming home on time."

"Did you drive?" I ask.

She shakes her head. "Bus."

"Then let me give you a ride home. We'll

listen to some tunes."

She crosses her arms. "You can give me a ride *near* my home."

I kiss her fast but soft and we head toward my car, which I bought with a combination of summer KFC income and a loan from Lee. We make out for a while in the car, but we get hit with the bright lights of one of those mall security guard cars, so she tells me to get going. Except for her giving me directions to where she lives, we don't talk, and somehow that's better. She finds a station she likes, sings along every now and then, but mostly just hangs on to my arm. "Pull over here," she whispers.

I pull into a subdivision that's got a few houses. We drive toward the back of it, where it's nice and dark. "I only got ten minutes before my bus is supposed to..."

I cut her off with a kiss so as not to waste a second. My car was built for speed on the open road, not romance in the front seat, so we do the best we can in the time and space.

When she has to go, I drop her on the main road outside of a nicer area than I live in. When my uncle gets his own store, maybe we can afford one of these dream houses too. Anything seems possible right now. Six months ago, I was acting stupid with Martel and Anton, heading down Dad's road, but now I got Ralisha—and a new attitude.

But I know the best way to stay on the path I'm on is to look at the ending point for the path I was following. Instead of heading home, I head east, toward Oak Park Heights.

It's not visiting hours or anything, so I drive around the outside of the prison and look at the thick walls, the barbed-wire fences, and the tall guard towers. It ain't a pretty sight. It's like the building was specifically designed to suck the life out of the men inside—and those of us on the outside too. "Prison takes everything from a man," Dad once said.

But I won't let it take everything from me. I'm gonna build a life out here, and I'm not gonna let anyone take it from me. If anybody tries, I'll fight to keep it. One way or another.

14

I don't feel like going home yet, so I take the back streets. To get my mind off Dad, I hook up my phone and blast some tunes. That helps. While my system doesn't rock as loud as the one in Martel's ride, I'm getting some serious shake. I'm singing along, leaning back, when I see it out of my rearview: flashing red lights. I turn down the music but I'm still shaking.

Before I roll down the window, I take a deep breath. I pull my ID from my Levis and wait. It seems way too long goes by before I hear a deep voice ask for "license and registration."

I hand my license to the officer—a youngish white guy with soul patch and a Woodbury PD shield. I start to reach for my registration in the glove box, but suddenly he starts yelling.

"Put your hands where I can see them!" He roars over the sound of his side-holster unbuckling. I do as I'm told. "Turn so I can see you." And I do that too. He can see me; I can see his angry white face and black pistol.

"Out of the car, now!" he yells, somehow even louder. I do that too. "On the ground."

"What did I do?"

"I said on the ground, on your knees, hands behind your head, and don't move a muscle."

He shines a flashlight right in my eyes and it blinds me for a second. Behind me, I sense he's shining that light and looking through the car for whatever it is he assumes I stole.

"What are you doing out here at this hour?" I'm on my knees, staring up at him.

"Seeing my girlfriend." Even as tense as this is, the image of Ralisha makes me smile.

"You think this is funny?" I squeeze my hands together hard against the back of my head. He starts talking about robberies in the neighborhood. "Know anything about that?"

"I don't live around here," I say, as if he doesn't know that.

"I do, and it's my job to protect these citizens from thugs and hoodlums."

"Can I go?" I speak into the ground.

"After I write you a ticket." He clicks his pen; it sounds like a trigger.

"For what, driving while black?" I snap. He doesn't say a word, just shines the flashlight in my face again. I think about moving my hands to block the light, but I can't risk it. I shut my eyes tight. I hear the sound of his footsteps and then the clatter of glass breaking.

"For driving with a broken tail light." He drops the ticket in front of me. I wait until he walks away before I stand up. And I wait until his intact tail lights are way out of view before I rip up the ticket.

***

"Why are you late?" Lee asks when I walk in the door. I saw that he'd called earlier, but I couldn't answer, having my hands behind my back and all.

"Where's Gramps?" I ask. "I want him to hear this too."

Lee looks puzzled, though Gramps and I have been getting along a little better since his talk in history class. Lee heads into the other room, and I turn to the fridge. When he comes back with Gramps, I'm seated at the table with three open beers, one for each of us.

"What's the story?" Lee asks. He says nothing about me drinking the beer. It's nasty. People must really love to get drunk if they drink this garbage. Why something so foul is legal and something as good as weed ain't—well, add that to the list of things that are seriously messed up.

While I explain what happened, I think about Gramps on Pettus Bridge in Selma in 1965. All those cops, all that yelling, all that hatred. And it seemed so long ago until tonight.

"You gotta pay the ticket, DeQuin," says Lee when I'm finished.

"But I didn't do anything wrong!"

"It's true," says Gramps. "They had no excuse to pull him over."

"Well, there's nothing we can do about that," snaps Lee. "No point getting yourself in more trouble now, DeQuin. Just pay the fine and move on. There's a saying: 'Get along, go along.'"

I notice Gramps jamming and twisting his cane into the floor like a drill. The sound launches a headache I haven't felt for almost a month.

"Just keep your head down," Lee's saying. "That's how you survive."

"Isn't that selling out?" I ask.

"Let me see," says Lee. "Pretty soon I'll be able to buy my own store, control my own future, and not have my boss, a white man with money, tell me what to do ever again. So you tell me. Is that selling out?"

Gramps shakes his head. "It's all about money with you, but back in—"

"No, Daddy, it's about respect," my uncle shoots back. "Every day I turn on the TV, turn on the radio, do I see the millions of black men like me playing by the rules? No, I see thug criminals, rappers getting arrested, and black men being made fun of all over the place." He finishes his beer. "And then I visit my brother, and I see a man who fits that image, and he didn't have to. He was like DeQuin once. A bright kid with attitude. And look what he turned into. Didn't have to happen. You stay out of trouble, work hard, then you get your chance."

Gramps looks at his own beer in disgust. "Sometimes a man can't stay out of trouble. Sometimes trouble is standing in his path."

Did I hear that wrong, or did Gramps just call me a man?

"Jimmie was a follower," Gramps says. "Both my sons are followers. He went along with the gang life. You, Lee, you went along with the quiet life. DeQuin ain't a follower."

"Well, he's still gotta pay that fine," says Lee, and the conversation is over.

My head feels like someone's taking a whack at it all over again. If I'm not a follower, what am I? If I can't fight and I can't run, what are my choices?

15

After last night, the only thing that'll make me feel better is seeing Ralisha. But it's Sunday, so I got twenty-four hours till I see her at school. I call her and we meet up in this little park a couple blocks away from her house.

"What's wrong, boo?" Ralisha asks. First I tell her about getting pulled over last night. But she can see that's not all that's bothering me.

I decide to be totally honest for the first time. I start with why I had to leave Harding. I've shown her the scar but never told the story of how I got beat up.

Now I tell her everything, from how I used to run with Martel and Anton through the night at the amusement park up until I got smacked in the back of the head. "For a long time I felt like it all came down to that moment in the parking lot, when I decided to run," I say. "I thought I made the wrong choice. But now I think—maybe when you're on the wrong path, there are no right choices. No matter what I did that night, it was gonna end bad. Hanging with Martel and Anton, following their lead all those years, that was my real mistake. But I'm done with all that. It's time to get serious."

"That's what I need, DeQuin," Ralisha says. "Too many fools and boys pretending to be men. I need somebody I can count on, somebody who will stand up and do the right thing."

"That's me, these days." I kiss her gently. "And now I get to ask you something. How come we been together all this time and you never had me to your house?"

Ralisha removes the phone from her back pocket, unlocks it, and taps the screen. "You're right. I've been afraid too," she says. "I guess it's time for you to meet my family."

Ralisha wraps one arm around the back of

my neck, pulling me tight. With the other she holds the phone and starts to flip through photos. "That's my moms and dads," she says and then pauses her thumb. "And this is my pride and joy. This is my son, Ramon."

PART THREE: MAY

16

"What you up to this weekend?" Ralisha asks me over the phone as I walk out with the closing crew after a busy night. Her tone's light and teasing, which is good to hear—a nice change from all the serious talks we've been having lately.

I'm still absorbing everything she's told me about her family over the past few months. Ramon's the reason she leaves school early every day. She goes to Harding in the morning, parents and does her online classes in the afternoon, and then works nights. It's a hard life, and she's been doing it for three years now, since Ramon was born. No wonder she don't have time for fools.

"I got this thing to go to for work on Saturday," I say. "My uncle's boss, the owner of the stores he supervises, has this big party every May for kids who work at his stores and are graduating from high school. He invites his senior team too, which includes my uncle Lee. And Lee always brings me. He wants me to dress up, look respectable."

"Well, you can't be disappointing your uncle," she says.

"Yeah, he's pretty uptight about it. He's planning on asking Mr. Richards if he can buy one of the stores."

"That's great, DeQuin. You sound really proud of him."

"Yeah, I guess I am." He stepped up to raise me, along with working hard on his career. I always think of myself as not really having a father. But I guess Lee's been my father. "Are you proud of your dad? And your mom? What do they do?" I ask.

There's a long pause before she says, "You

can ask them yourself. I'd like you to have dinner with them, me, and Ramon on Sunday for Mother's Day."

It's like a big old window just swung open and let in a gust of fresh air. "I'd love that, baby," I say.

We talk a little more before she needs to go. My head's still spinning from the thought of meeting her folks when I stop dead in my tracks.

There's Martel leaning against my ride.

He steps forward, extends his arms, wraps me in a hug, gives me a bump, another hug. It feels weird, the old routine. I flash to him sitting behind the wheel of his Jeep last September. *It's all good. We cool.* I'd wanted to believe him so bad. Even after, when I woke up in the hospital, when I heard Martel's and Anton's side of the story from Lee and the cops—even then I'd tried to believe it.

But I ain't walking around with my eyes closed anymore. I take a step back from Martel and wait.

"Hey, man," he says. "I knew you wouldn't take my calls, but I needed to see you, tell you something." We lean on the side of my car.

"What is it? I have homework." Not a lie. Armstrong High is kicking my butt something fierce.

"Look, it's been a while and a lot's gone down," he starts. He won't look at me when he talks. "I'm working a program now, making amends and such. I need to make peace with everyone I hurt, especially you, DeQuin."

I've waited for this. I've dreaded it. I need to hear it. "How did you hurt me, Martel?"

"We were serious angry at you, so we taught you a lesson about bailing on friends." He glances at me out of the corner of his eye. "I figured you knew it was us."

I rub my head; my finger lingers on the scar. "Yeah, I was pretty sure."

"But you never said anything to the cops."

"I might be chicken, but I didn't snitch."

"I owe you. And for real, I didn't mean for you to get hurt that bad. We were just trying to make a point."

"There's better ways to make a point than cracking somebody's skull."

"I know that now," Martel says. "Times change, I guess."

I nod.

"So. We good?"

I shake my head. "We ain't good...but we ain't bad. It takes courage to man up and confess like this, and I appreciate it. But we're not friends."

Martel nods. "I feel you, DeQuin. A man's got to do what a man's got to do."

I bump him again and nod in agreement. Except, for so many things in my life, I still don't know what it is a man would do.

17

"You know, Ralisha, I'm seventeen years old, and I've been dressing myself just fine for years," I say as we walk out of yet another clothing store at Maplewood Mall.

"If you're coming to my house, you're gonna clean up and look right, not wearing no ratty old Levis and a LeBron jersey and such," she argues back, but in a fun way. That's one of the things I like about Ralisha, she can take it and give it out. "I got fashion sense, DeQuin. You look most days like you been dressed by a blind man."

"Maybe I'll just wear my KFC uniform."

"Yeah, right. Speaking of KFC, you need to dress nice for that party, don't you? So if you buy a suit, you'll get to wear it twice in one week. That's a good investment, DeQuin."

"Look at you bustin' out the vocab from econ class," I tease her.

But she doesn't let me get her off track. "Why don't we go over to Woodbury? They got some of those nice places like Joseph Banks and stuff. You'd look sharp in those, I bet."

I don't tell her that I want to avoid Woodbury. "Too expensive."

"Tell you what." She gets close to me, whispers in my ear. "You know what other store is there? Victoria's Secret. Maybe I'll have to try on some things for you to see."

The keys are out of my pocket and in my hand so fast it defies physics.

***

At the fancy men's suit store, I feel out of place in a hundred ways. First, because I've never been in a store like this with clothes this expensive. Second, because ain't nobody in the store as young as me and Ralisha. And third, of course, ain't nobody in the store looks like us, except maybe a lady working the register who's spent too much time under a tanning lamp.

"At least buy a nice tie," Ralisha says. "I'll even tie it for you."

Before I can answer, some older guy with a gray beard comes over. "Are you finding everything you need?" he asks. I kind of nod and smile but don't answer. "You're sure?"

"Yeah, we're fine." But he's not moving. He's right next to me. It's weird.

Ralisha points to a sales rack, so we head over there.

"All this merchandise is on sale," the guy says.

"Thanks," I mumble. I glance toward the exit. There's an older white security guard staring at me.

I grab two shirts from the sale rack and head for the back where I saw the dressing rooms. Ralisha has to run to keep up with my long legs.

"Do you need some help with those?" the guy asks, but I blow past him.

I go into the dressing room, hang up the shirts, and stare at my reflection. The shirts all look wrong on me. When I come out of the dressing room, as I could've guessed, the old guy's waiting for me. I hand him his overpriced shirts and say, "You don't have to follow me."

"I don't need any problems with you people," he says.

"But we're not causing problems," Ralisha says. "All we want to do is shop."

"And all I want to do is make sure that nothing happens in my store," the guy answers with a straight face. "Maybe it would be best for everyone if you just leave."

"No." And I'm with Gramps on the Pettus Bridge.

"No." And Ralisha is there with me. I got backup.

"I'm calling the police," he says and pulls out his phone.

"We didn't do anything, so I'm not sure what you're going tell them," Ralisha says.

"I'm asking you to leave. If you don't, then I guess you're trespassing."

I look at Ralisha. She's still with me. "We're standing our ground."

The guy sighs, puts his phone back in his pocket and walks away. We've called his bluff.

"OK then," Ralisha says to me, all casual. "Let's find you a suit."

18

"Can we go soon?" I ask Lee. It's not just that I hate wearing the suit. It's everything else about Lee's boss's party at this country club in Woodbury. I got a change of clothes in the car that I'm itching to get into as soon as possible. Lee wouldn't let me bring Ralisha—he didn't say why and I didn't ask—but he's dropping me at Maplewood Mall after.

"DeQuin, this is a big deal for me, especially this year," Lee says. "I don't recall you raising a fuss last year. In fact, last year, all I remember you doing was eating plates of food."

I don't say, *Well, Lee, that's because I was high last year.* Instead, I head for the buffet, which is loaded with nice food, instead of the KFC stuff we practically live on.

I load up my plate and look for a place to sit. The only table with an opening is with a bunch of white crew members. I introduce myself, mention my uncle, and join the conversation.

"So what colleges are you all going to?" I ask. Maybe I can learn something for when I have to decide next year. Gramps wants me to go to the University of Alabama, and considering how much he complains about everything in Minnesota, he'll probably want to come south with me.

"Um, I'm not going to college," replies a short fat white guy with a name tag that says *Benny*. "I'm going full-time the day school is over."

"Same," adds the girl, named Brittney of course. "I might take a class at the community college."

A couple more talk about going into the Army, and finally one girl says, "I'm going to St. Cloud State, but honestly, that's mainly to play hockey."

"Serious? None of you's going out of state, or even to the U?" I ask, all shocked.

"Well, not all of us have it easy." Benny nods toward Lee, who stands next to Mr. Richards.

I fight the urge to roll my eyes. "Easy?"

"Yeah, DeQuin, easy," Brittney says in a tone like she's spitting on me. "Not all of us got lucky enough to be the son of the general manager."

I barely register that she called me Lee's son. I'm too busy chewing on the rest of what she said. There ain't been too many times in my life I felt lucky. I want to ask Brittney if she's got a dad behind bars, if she's been dragging that chain most of her life. I want to ask her if she had her skull smashed in by people she thought were her friends. Seems like the whole world's ready to judge me without knowing nothing about me.

I catch sight of Lee across the room. He's watching me—probably praying I don't say something to embarrass him. *Just keep your head down, DeQuin*, I bet he's thinking. *Play nice.*

But I can't do it. I can't be who Lee wants me to be, or even who Gramps thinks I am.

I pick up my plate, dump the fancy food in the garbage, and go over to Lee. "Be right back," I say. "I forgot something in the car." Myself.

In the car's backseat I lose the suit and get back into real clothes: jeans and a hoodie. Then I set off down the wide streets of Whitebury. I gotta walk it off.

"So how late you working? I need to see you," I say to Ralisha as soon as she picks up. "I'm feelin' all messed up right now and—"

"Hey, you, what are you doing out here?" I hear a male voice call out from behind me.

I just keep talking to Ralisha. She's excited about me meeting her son and the rest of her family next Sunday. I focus on her words, trying to ignore the harsh voice yelling at me for no reason.

"I said what are you doing out there?" The voice is deep, angry, scared.

Ralisha breaks off. "What's that noise?"

"Some guy's yelling at me." I pull my hood over my head to block out the sound.

"For what?" she asks.

"He thinks I'm Tiger Woods and wants my

autograph."

"Freeze!" the guy shouts almost in my ear. "This is your last warning."

I turn. It's no Woodbury PD, just a pudgy guy in a polo shirt—security guard, maybe, for the golf club, or maybe some neighborhood watch thing. "What's going on?" Ralisha asks.

My body tenses: do I flee, fight or freeze? "Nothing's going on," I say into the phone. I take a step toward the guy. "What's your problem? Why—"

But I stop when I see it.

"DeQuin, what's going on?" Ralisha repeats, frantic now.

What's going on is that I'm staring down into the mouth of a pistol.

19

Blood drips down, staining my shoes. Some of it's my blood, from where the guard bashed my eyebrow open with the side of his gun. Some of it's his blood, which splattered everywhere when I knocked out half his teeth.

The wail of the sirens from the police cars and ambulance makes my ears thrum, while the flashing lights from the vehicles blind me.

"Let me see your hands!" the cop shouts. The same cop who broke my tail light? Sure looks like it. As I hold my hands out in front of me, I try to stop them from shaking.

Another cop with a camera takes pictures. Once that's done, an EMT checks me out.

"I think my hand's broken." I don't ask about the guard's jaw. I know that's broken.

"We'll fix him up after we book him." The cop talks about me like I'm not there. He motions for me to put my hands behind me. I grit my teeth against the pain. The cuffs click together. It reminds me of the sound the doors at the prison make, a sound I'll be hearing soon enough.

"I didn't do anything," I say, head held high, defiant.

I start to tell the cop about the guard waving his gun, coming at me. Even as I'm spilling my guts, I can tell he's not listening. This cop made up his mind about me the first time he saw me.

He pushes me hard toward his car. "You can tell it to the judge in the morning."

"I wanna call home," I say as I squeeze into the backseat. He doesn't protect my head.

"You can call your daddy from jail," says the cop.

"My dad's already *in* jail," I snap before I can stop myself. "I said I want to call home."

The cop smirks. "Or maybe we can just arrange a family reunion."

I bite the insides of my mouth to keep from saying anything else. They already saw me as a criminal, and now they're seeing me as my father's son.

The cop slams the car door. Seconds later, like a delayed echo, the door on the ambulance slams. I'm off to jail and the guard's off to the hospital, but that's on him. He gave me no choice. No more fleeing or freezing. I fought, not to hurt others, like Dad did, but to defend myself. I stood my ground. No matter what these cops say or do, they won't make me regret that.

The car starts to pull away, and I brace myself for whatever's coming next.

AFTERWORD

As of 2014, it's estimated that more than 2.7 million children in the United States have a parent behind bars. About one in five of those kids are teenagers. While having parents in prison presents challenges at any age, it may be particularly hard for teenagers, as they try to find their way in the world.

The *Locked Out* series explores the realities of parental incarceration through the eyes of teens dealing with it. These stories are fictional, but the experiences that Patrick Jones writes about are daily life for many youths.

The characters deal with racism, stigma,

shame, sadness, confusion, and isolation—common struggles for children with parents in prison. Many teens are forced to move from their homes, schools, or communities as their families cope with their parents' incarcerations.

These extra challenges can affect teens with incarcerated parents in different ways. Kids often struggle in school – they are at increased risk for skipping school, feeling disconnected from classmates, and failing classes. They act out and test boundaries. And they're prone to taking risks, like using substances or engaging in other illegal activities.

In addition, studies have shown that youth who are involved in the juvenile justice system are far more likely than their peers to have a parent in the criminal justice system. In Minnesota, for example, boys in juvenile correctional facilities are ten times more likely than boys in public schools to have a parent currently incarcerated. This cycle of incarceration is likely caused by many factors. These include systemic differences in the distribution of wealth and resources, as well as bias within policies and practices.

The *Locked Out* series offers a glimpse into this complex world. While the books don't sugarcoat reality, each story offers a window of hope. The teen characters have a chance to thrive despite difficult circumstances. These books highlight the positive forces that make a difference in teens' lives: a loving, consistent caregiver; other supportive, trustworthy adults; meaningful connections at school; and participation in sports or other community programs. Indeed, these are the factors in teens' lives that mentoring programs around the country aim to strengthen, along with federal initiatives such as My Brother's Keeper, launched by President Obama.

This series serves as a reminder that just because a parent is locked up, it doesn't mean kids need to be locked out.

—Dr. Rebecca Shlafer
Department of Pediatrics,
University of Minnesota

AUTHOR ACKNOWLEDGMENTS

Thanks to Dr. Rebecca J. Shlafer and members of her research team for reading and commenting on this manuscript. Thanks to Raven from South St. Paul Community Learning Center and Dan Marcou for their manuscript reviews.

ABOUT THE AUTHOR

Patrick Jones is the author of more than twenty-five novels for teens. He has also written two nonfiction books about combat sports: *The Main Event*, on professional wrestling, and *Ultimate Fighting*, on mixed martial arts. He has spoken to students at more than one hundred alternative schools and has worked with incarcerated teens and adults for more than a decade. Find him on the web at www.connectingya.com and on Twitter: @PatrickJonesYA.

THE ALTERNATIVE

FAILING CLASSES.
DROPPING OUT.
JAIL TIME.

When it seems like there are no other options left,
Rondo Alternative High School might just be the
last chance a student needs.

BARRIER
PATRICK JONES

BRIDGE
PATRICK JONES

CONTROLLED
PATRICK JONES

OUTBURST
PATRICK JONES

TARGET
PATRICK JONES